NICKOMMOH!

A Thanksgiving Celebration

by JACKIE FRENCH KOLLER   •   *illustrated by* MARCIA SEWALL

Atheneum Books for Young Readers

The author wishes to thank Dr. Ella Sekatau, Tribal Ethnohistorian of the Narragansett Indian Tribe, for her invaluable contribution of time and knowledge.

Editor's note: The Native American words and other expressions of specific interest that are italicized in this book are defined in a glossary at the end.

Atheneum Books for Young Readers
An imprint of Simon & Schuster Children's Publishing Division
1230 Avenue of the Americas
New York, New York 10020

Book design by Nina Barnett
The text of this book is set in Garth Graphic.
The illustrations are rendered in scratchboard and gouache.

Printed in Singapore
10 9 8 7 6 5 4 3 2 1

Library of Congress Cataloging-in-Publication Data
Koller, Jackie French.
Nickommoh! : A Thanksgiving celebration / by Jackie French Koller; illustrated by Marcia Sewall.—1st ed.
p. cm.
Summary: Describes a typical Narragansett Nickommoh, or harvest celebration, as it has been performed since before the arrival of the first Pilgrims in New England.
ISBN 0-689-81094-6
1. Narragansett Indians—Social life and customs—Juvenile literature.
2. Thanksgiving Day—Juvenile literature. 3. Indians of North America—New England—Social life and customs—Juvenile literature. [1. Narragansett Indians—Rhode Island—Social life and customs. 2. Indians of North America—Rhode Island—Social life and customs.] I. Sewall, Marcia, ill.
E99.N16K65   1999
394.2649'089973—dc21   97-37087   CIP   AC

To Firefly Song of Wind Sekatau,
and to her People, the Narragansett
—J. K.

For Douglas, Little One
—M. S.

Kautantawwitt, the Creator, is pleased with his People. They have cared well for his gifts of Corn and Bean and Squash. In the early warmth of *Sequan*, when the oak leaves were the size of a mouse's ear, the People planted. All through the long, hot days of *Quaqusquan*, the growing time, the People tended the Creator's gifts, keeping weeds from their feet, carrying water to quench their thirst, and shooing away mischievous *Kaukant*, the crow.

Now frost lies thick on the fields at dawn, and the winged ones pass overhead in great numbers, calling out their good-byes. It is *Taqountikeeswush,* the Moon of the Falling Leaves. The Creator's gifts have been harvested, dried, and tucked away in *auqunnash* in the bosom of Earth Mother. They will provide for the People all through the long, cold months to come, the long, cold months of *Papone.* It is time, now. Time for the People to come together, together to give thanks.

NICKOMMOH!

From villages far and near they come, their *mocussinass* treading silently on the footsteps of the Grandfathers, following the paths the Grandfathers walked, walked since the days *When the Animals Were Big* and the Old Ones hunted the *Stiff-Legged Bear.* With joyful greetings they come together, together to give thanks.

NICKOMMOH!

The men cut poles and set them in the earth, bend them
over and bind them tight. Bind them to make the *Qunnekamuck,*

the great lodge that will hold the People, the People who come together,
together to give thanks.

NICKOMMOH!

The women cover the poles with bark, and line them inside with fine, woven mats. Mats to make the Qunnekamuck beautiful, mats to keep it snug and dry. Fires are lit to keep the People warm and to cook the food that the People will eat. Venison and turkey the People will eat, and beans and squash and clams, with good, thick *nasaump* puddings and sweet cakes of berries and corn. With prayers of thanksgiving, the People will eat.

NICKOMMOH!

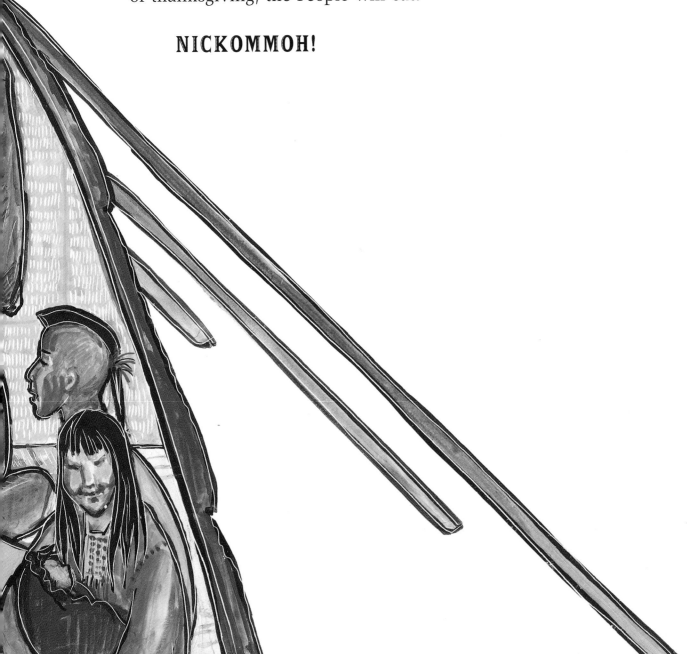

Women cook and talk and laugh while children run and tumble. Men gather in a *gaming arbor* to play at games of chance, holding tight their *thunderbolts,* cheering as the stones are tossed. Others compete in games of skill, like *spear-the-disk* or *tug-of-war.* In time the games grow lively and loud, lively and loud and full of fun. The women and children join in.

NICKOMMOH!

When the day grows old and sun rests on the shoulders of the western hills, the sweat lodges are prepared. Into the *Pesuponck* the People go, leaving their clothes at the door. Wearing only the raiment the Creator gave them, the People enter in. Close in a *sacred circle* they sit, to talk and smoke and sweat. To be made pure of body and pure of spirit, the People sit and sweat.

NICKOMMOH!

Now out of the lodges the People run. Into the river they plunge. The water pricks like needles of ice, burns like tongues of fire, washing away every impurity, making the People strong. Now the People's bodies glow. Their spirits are at peace. One by one they drift away. Soon the Dance will begin.

NICKOMMOH!

The People anoint themselves with oil. They comb and dress their hair. From Kautantawwitt's sacred palette they choose colors to paint their skins. The Creator's sacred colors they choose—*Msqui, Wesaui, Mowi-sucki.* Earth red, Sun yellow, Night black.

NICKOMMOH!

In garments of deerskin the People dress, in fine turkey-feather capes. Their best mocussinass they put on their feet. *Wompampeage* belts ring their waists. With Kautantawwitt's jewels they adorn

themselves, the Creator's sacred jewels—bright feathers, dyed quills, gems of stone, claw, and bone, beads of shining shell.

NICKOMMOH!

Now Moon Sister wakes and draws her star blanket across the sky. Beneath the blanket the People come together, into the Sacred Circle. With glad hearts and prayers of thanksgiving, the People come,

bearing gifts so that widows may eat and orphans grow strong,
because all belong. All belong to the Sacred Family of the People.

NICKOMMOH!

Drums speak in stirring beats and the People lift their voices in song. Joyful songs of thanksgiving, soft songs of love, sad songs of longing for those who are gone. Songs of war, songs of peace, songs of living and dying and living again, living again in the Great House of Kautantawwitt.

NICKOMMOH!

Moving in circles the People dance, feeling Earth Mother's heart beat beneath their feet. Quick dances of joy they dance, whirling and twirling and stomping. Bold dances of war they dance, shrieking and howling and leaping. Slow dances of love they dance, rhythmically

swaying and stepping. Young people cast shy glances as they pass.

Firelight flickers in their eyes and turns their skin to gold.

Kautantawwitt's sacred firelight shines upon the People.

NICKOMMOH!

Old ones nod with lidded eyes. Small ones sleep in loving arms.
Moon Sister creeps across the sky. And the People dance on. Up, up
into the night their voices rise, gathered by Brother Wind and carried
to the ears of the Creator.

"Thank you, Kautantawwitt!" the People cry. "Thank you for
your love!"

In his Great House in the Southwest, Kautantawwitt smiles. He hears the prayers of his Children and holds them in his heart.

"Peace, my Children," he whispers.

And the People dance on.

NICKOMMOH!

AUTHOR'S NOTE

Long before the first Pilgrim set foot in the New World, Native Americans were celebrating rites of thanksgiving, thirteen a year, in fact—one for each lunar month. In addition, several times a year larger celebrations were held, celebrations that were both religious and social in nature. On these occasions, feasting, gaming, and dancing accompanied the religious ceremonies. *Nickommoh* was the name given by the Narragansett Indian Tribe of present-day Rhode Island to these celebrations. A Nickommoh might be small, with just a couple of villages coming together, or large, with thousands coming from far and wide. The largest Nickommohs were usually held in the fall, to celebrate the harvest, and in the winter, to break the boredom of that cold, harsh season.

These feasts take their name from the word *Nickommoh,* which means "give away" or "exchange." During the feasts a giveaway dance was held. People would give away any extra food, furs, clothing, etc., that they might have accumulated. These gifts were distributed by the sachem (king) to widows, orphans, or any who were in need. In Narragansett society, the more a man gave away, the more highly he was respected.

The first Thanksgiving of the Pilgrims of Plymouth was actually more like the traditional Native American harvest Nickommoh than like the holiday we celebrate today. Held out-of-doors, it lasted for three days and included gaming, feasting, and contests of skill. Though history books have traditionally credited the Pilgrims with initiating the "first" Thanksgiving, it is obvious that the Native People contributed richly to the event.

Although the Native American words in this story are from the Narragansett language, the celebration they depict is much like celebrations held all over New England before the white man came, and in many places, long after. The Native American powwow of today is descended from this type of celebration.

The fact that Native American people do "dance on" today, despite hundreds of years of overt and covert attempts by the United States government to usurp their lands and their native identities, is a tribute to the tenacity and deep spirituality of America's indigenous peoples.

GLOSSARY

The Native American words in this book are from the language of the Narragansett people of present-day Rhode Island. The spellings are drawn from *Roger Williams Key into the Language of America.*

Auqunnash: Pits dug into the earth and lined with mats. Baskets of dried foods were stored in these for winter use.

Gaming Arbor (Puttuckquapuonck): An arbor consisting of four poles sixteen to twenty feet high, set up in a square. Strings of wampum and other valued possessions were hung from the poles. Men then gambled for the prizes.

Kaukant: Crow, the sacred bird of the Narragansett. Legend tells that Crow brought the seeds of Corn, Bean, and Squash to the Narragansett from Kautantawwitt's Garden in the Southwest. The Narragansett people would shoo Kaukant away from their fields at growing time, but never harm her.

Kautantawwitt: God, the Creator, who gave a spirit to all of his creations, animate and inanimate.

Mocussinass: Soft deerskin shoes.

Msqui, Wesaui, Mowi-sucki: The colors red, yellow, and black. The Narragansett used these and other colors to paint their bodies and faces. They painted for ceremonies and for war, but also for everyday adornment. It is likely, in fact, that the European term "red man" referred not to skin color, but rather to the favored red paint used in this practice.

Nasaump: Cornmeal, boiled in water to a thick pudding. Nasaump was the staple food of the Narragansett diet.

Nickommoh: A celebrational gathering.

Papone: Winter

Pesuponck: A sweat lodge. Usually a small hut or cave, six to eight feet across, near a stream or riverbank. A fire is built either inside or outside the cave and stones are heated until white-hot, then the fire is allowed to die out. If the stones are outside, they are rolled into the cave. Then ten to twenty people crowd in. Closing the opening over, they sit and sweat for an hour or more. Narragansetts took sweats frequently, often daily, as a means of cleansing and purification. They were performed before hunts, journeys, plantings, etc., day or night.

Quaqusquan: Summer

Qunnekamuck: A ceremonial longhouse, sometimes one hundred to two hundred feet long. Narragansetts lived in permanent communal longhouses in sheltered inland areas during the winter. In the summer they moved to breezy areas along the shore and built smaller, individual family dwellings.

Sacred Circle: Native American peoples believe that the Power of the World works in circles, and therefore the circle is a sacred shape. When Native American people gather for ceremonies, dances, etc., it is in a circle.

Sequan: Spring

Spear-the-Disk: A flat stone, rounded to a disk, was sent rolling on its edge while players hurled eight-foot poles, trying to land them as close as possible to where the disk would come to rest.

Stiff-Legged Bear: The great woolly mammoth

Taqountikeeswush: Harvest Month (October)

Thunderbolts: Crystalline stones found in the ground near trees that had been struck by lightning, thought to bring luck.

Tug-of-War: Players formed two teams and stretched a rope between them, marking the midline on the ground. On a signal, both teams would begin to pull, and the first to pull the other across the midline was the winner. Often, to make the game more interesting, the rope would be stretched across a stream, ravine, or mud bog.

When the Animals Were Big: The Pleistocene Era, when the great woolly mammoth, giant elk, caribou, musk ox, saber-toothed tiger, giant beaver, and an immense Kodiak-like species of bear inhabited New England.

Wompampeage (Wampum): Purple and white beads made from quahog shell, used for adornment and also as money. The purple beads were rarer and worth about three times as much as the white.